A Person Can Be...

Written by
Kerri Kokias

Illustrated by
Carey Sookocheff

KIDS CAN PRESS

A person can be ...

Naughty and nice.

Curious and cautious.

Busy and bored.

Homesick and adventurous.

Wrong and sorry.

Imperfect and treasured.

Careful and clumsy.

Big and still snuggly.

Unlucky and lucky.

Small and strong.

Safe and scared.

Proud and embarrassed.

Talented and shy.

Loved and lonely.

Alone and not lonely.

Excited and nervous.

Brave and afraid.

Sad and smiling.

Full and hungry.

Hungry and not hungry.

Different and ...

the same.

To Dave, a dreamer and a doer — K.K.

For my mom, Laura, who always thought I could be anything I wanted to be — C.S.

Published in Canada and the U.S. by Kids Can Press Ltd.
25 Dockside Drive, Toronto, ON M5A 0B5

Kids Can Press is a Corus Entertainment Inc. company.

www.kidscanpress.com

The artwork in this book was rendered traditionally using acrylic gouache and drawing pencil.
The text is set in Nouveau Crayon.

Edited by Yasemin Uçar and Debbie Rogosin
Designed by Andrew Dupuis

Printed and bound in Buji, Shenzhen, China, in 3/2022 by WKT Company

CM 22 0 9 8 7 6 5 4 3 2 1

FSC
www.fsc.org
MIX
Paper from
responsible sources
FSC® C010256

LIBRARY AND ARCHIVES CANADA CATALOGUING IN PUBLICATION

Title: A person can be ... / written by Kerri Kokias ; illustrated by Carey Sookocheff.
Names: Kokias, Kerri, author. | Sookocheff, Carey, 1972– illustrator.
Identifiers: Canadiana 20210359307 | ISBN 9781525304873 (hardcover)
Subjects: LCSH: Characters and characteristics — Juvenile literature. | LCSH: Personality — Juvenile
literature. | LCSH: Emotions — Juvenile literature.
Classification: LCC BF831 .K65 2022 | DDC j155.2 — dc23

Kids Can Press gratefully acknowledges that the land on which our office is located is the traditional territory of many nations,
including the Mississaugas of the Credit, the Anishnabeg, the Chippewa, the Haudenosaunee and the Wendat peoples,
and is now home to many diverse First Nations, Inuit and Métis peoples.

We thank the Government of Ontario, through Ontario Creates; the Ontario Arts Council; the Canada Council for the Arts;
and the Government of Canada for supporting our publishing activity.